The Story of Our Ponies

Do you love ponies? Be a Pony Pal!

Look for these Pony Pal books:

Pony Pals

The Story of Our Ponies

Jeanne Betancourt

illustrated by Paul Bachem

A
LITTLE APPLE
PAPERBACK

SCHOLASTIC INC.
New York Toronto London Auckland Sydney

ISBN 0-590-86631-1

12 11 10 9 8 7 6 5 4   3 4 5 6 7 8 9/0

Printed in the U.S.A.   40

First Scholastic printing, May 1997

Thank you to Susan Houle of Wellspring Farm, Catherine Mack of Aladdin Connemaras, and Joan Stracks and her students in the Pegasus Therapeutic Riding Program.

This Pony Pal Super Special is dedicated to my super editor and special Pony Pal, Helen Perelman.

Contents

The Story of Our Ponies

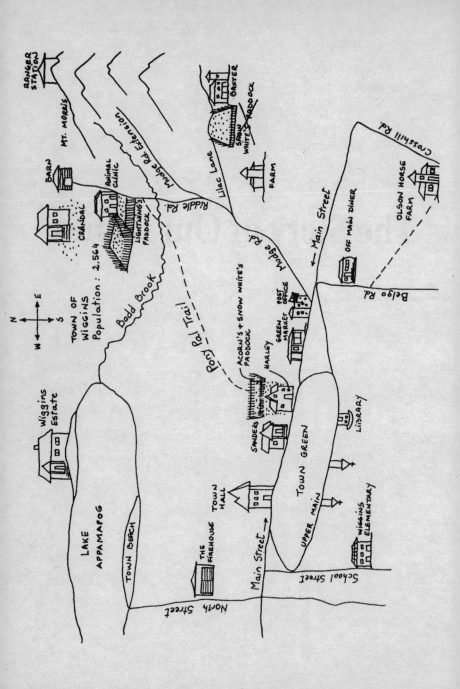

Snowflake

Lulu Sanders was finished packing her saddlebag for a Pony Pal barn sleepover. From her bedroom window, Lulu could see the backyard paddock that she shared with Anna Harley. Anna was trying to catch her pony, Acorn, and the Shetland pony was being very stubborn. Lulu opened the window and yelled out to Anna, "I'll be right there!"

In the yard, Anna had a new idea to catch Acorn. She walked over to Lulu's pony. "Okay, Snow White," she said. "Time to get ready for a trail ride." Anna led Snow White to the pony shelter and gave her a carrot. Soon, Acorn trotted over to them and nuzzled Anna's shoulder for attention.

"I knew you'd be jealous, Acorn," Anna said with a laugh.

Lulu ran across the yard toward Anna and the two ponies. "I have the best news!" she told Anna. She patted Snow White's smooth white neck. "It's great news for you, too, Snow White."

"What?" asked Anna.

"Mrs. Baxter just called me. Snow White's first owners are friends of the Baxters. They're coming to visit them," Lulu said.

"That's great," said Anna.

"But the best part is that they're going to have Snow White's *son* with them."

"What's the colt's name?" asked Anna.

"Snowflake," answered Lulu. "But he's not a colt anymore. He's four years old."

"Snowflake is a perfect name for Snow

White's son," said Anna. "Can we see him, too?"

"Mrs. Baxter said to come tomorrow morning," said Lulu. "It's going to be so much fun. I can't wait to tell Pam."

The two friends saddled up their ponies and rode out of the paddock onto Pony Pal Trail. The mile-and-a-half trail led through the woods to Pam Crandal's place. The Pony Pals used the trail to go back and forth to one another's houses.

Anna and Lulu loved to go to the Crandals' for sleepovers. Pam's mother was a riding teacher and her father was a veterinarian. Lulu thought that Pam was lucky that both her parents were so interested in animals.

Lulu's mother and father loved animals, too. But Lulu's mother died when Lulu was four years old. Her father studied and wrote about wild animals all over the world. Lulu used to travel with him. Now she stayed in Wiggins with her grandmother Sanders. Lulu missed being with her dad all the time, but she loved being a Pony Pal.

Pam and her pony Lightning were waiting for Anna and Lulu in the field at the end of the trail. Lulu told Pam about Snow White's first owners and Snowflake.

"That's great," said Pam. "You can ask them all about Snow White's life."

"Ask them if they have any pictures of Snow White when she was little," said Anna. "That'd be so cute to see."

"I will," said Lulu. "And I'm going to write down what they tell me."

"You should write about your adventures with Snow White, too," said Pam.

"Write about when you found her caught in that barbed wire," said Anna.

"You'll be writing Snow White's whole life story," said Pam.

"It will be a biography," said Lulu. "I'll call it *Snow White's Story.*"

Anna and Lulu let their ponies run free with Lightning. The three ponies galloped together across the sunny field. Lightning whinnied to show how happy she was to be with her Pony Pals.

"I wish I knew all about Lightning's past," said Pam. "All I know is that she was in a lot of horse shows."

"You could find out more about her," said Lulu. "Talk to the people you bought her from. Then you could write Lightning's story."

"Acorn had a lot of owners," Anna said. "But the only one I know is Tommy Rand."

"Poor Acorn!" exclaimed Pam.

The Pony Pals didn't like Tommy Rand. He was a mean-acting eighth-grader who liked to pick on younger kids — especially the Pony Pals.

"You should find Acorn's other owners," said Pam. "Then you could write Acorn's story."

"If we all write the stories of our ponies," added Lulu, "it would be a Pony Pal Project. That would be so much fun."

"Writing isn't fun," moaned Anna. Anna

was dyslexic and it was hard for her to work with letters.

"You can put lots of drawings in your story, Anna," said Lulu. "You're a great artist."

"And we'll help you with the spelling," added Pam.

"Okay," said Anna. "I'll write Acorn's story. What do we do first?"

"We need to be detectives and ask lots of questions," said Pam.

"Then we'll write down what we learn about our ponies," said Lulu.

"My mother has a whole pile of notebooks," said Pam. "I bet she'll let us each have one."

Mrs. Crandal thought that writing stories about their ponies was a great idea. She gave each of the girls a special pad and pencil.

After dinner the girls sat on their favorite rock near the paddock and talked about their Pony Pal Project.

"Let's make a list of all the things we want to know about our ponies," said Pam.

1. Where was my pony born?
2. Who were the parents (dam and sire)?
3. What was my pony like when she was a foal?
4. Who has owned or leased my pony?
5. How long did my pony live with them?
6. Why did they sell my pony?

After the Pony Pals finished the list they said good night to their ponies and went to the barn office. They played checkers for a while and talked about their Pony Pal Project. Finally, they slipped into their sleeping bags and said good night to one another.

Pam scratched a mosquito bite on her forehead. It reminded her of the upside-down heart on Lightning's forehead. She wondered if Lightning's marking showed from the day she was born. She added that question to her list.

From her sleeping bag, Anna saw the night sky. She recognized the Big Dipper. Anna wished that there was a group of stars that made the outline of Acorn's head. That's how much she loved him. She hoped that Acorn's other owners were nicer than Tommy Rand.

Lulu thought about Snow White's re-union with her son. She couldn't wait to meet Snowflake and Snow White's first owner. Lulu wondered what she would find out about her pony. Lulu looked over at her new Pony Pal notebook. She couldn't wait to fill up the pages.

A Reunion

Pam was the first Pony Pal to wake up the next morning. Pam loved getting up early. She dressed quietly and did her barn chores. When Anna and Lulu got up, the three girls fed their ponies. Then they went to the house for breakfast.

Mrs. Crandal was sitting at the big, round kitchen table eating her breakfast. She told the Pony Pals that there were muffins and plenty of cereal and fruit. "Help yourselves," she added.

"Mom, I want to ask you some questions

about Lightning for my Pony Pal Project," Pam said.

"Lulu and I will make breakfast while you interview your mother," Anna told Pam.

"I only have a minute, honey," Mrs. Crandal said. "I have to get out to the barn."

Pam sat across from her mother and opened her Pony Pal notebook. "I'll be quick," she said. "What's the name of the farm where we bought Lightning?"

"Echo Farm in Pine Plains, New York," Pam's mother answered. Pam wrote that down in her pad.

"Who owns Echo Farm?" Pam asked.

"Richard O'Connor," Mrs. Crandal said. Pam wrote that down, too.

"Did they give us any papers when we bought her?" asked Pam.

"Certainly," Mrs. Crandal said. "We have Lightning's registration papers."

Pam told her mother that she wanted to see the papers. "I'll look for them," said

11

Mrs. Crandal. "But now I have to go saddle up Splash for my first riding lesson."

"Thanks for the help, Mom," Pam said. She closed the notebook.

After breakfast the Pony Pals rode over to the Baxters' to see Snowflake and meet Snow White's first owner. Lulu and Snow White took the lead along Lilac Lane. As Snow White trotted around the big turn in the dirt road, Lulu spotted a big gray pony grazing in the Baxters' paddock. She halted Snow White and waited for Pam and Anna to catch up.

Lulu pointed. "There he is," she said excitedly. "Snow White's son."

"How come he's not white?" Anna asked.

"Ponies aren't born white," explained Pam. "They start out a color and turn white slowly. It can take years."

"I bet Snowflake will be all white someday," said Anna.

"Let's go up to the house and tell the Baxters that we're here," said Lulu.

The Pony Pals rode up to the big yellow

house. Rema Baxter and a tall, dark-haired boy came out to meet them. The Pony Pals didn't like Rema very much. Rema thought she was a big deal because she was fourteen years old and went to boarding school. And she wasn't nice to Lulu when Lulu bought Snow White from her.

The Pony Pals dismounted and said hello to Rema and the older boy.

"I'm Mark Johnson," he said. Mark ran his hands along Snow White's neck and looked in her eyes. "Hi there, Snow White."

"I won lots of ribbons with Snow White," Rema told Mark. She gave Lulu a phony smile. "How are you treating my horse, Lulu?"

"Snow White is a *pony*," said Anna sharply.

"Lulu is great with Snow White, Rema," added Pam. "You know that."

Mark smiled at Lulu. "So you're Snow White's new owner," he said. "Isn't Snow White a great ride?"

"The best," agreed Lulu. "And she loves to go on trail rides."

"Snowflake is already bigger than Snow White," Mark said. "I thought he'd be."

"Do you remember when Snowflake was born?" asked Pam.

"I do," Mark said. "I even remember when Snow White was born." He scratched Snow White's head. "Snow White was always my favorite."

"How come you sold her then?" asked Lulu.

"He probably got too old for ponies," said Rema. "Like me."

"I would have kept Snow White forever if I could," said Mark. "But it's our business to sell ponies. Now it's time to sell Snowflake. That's why we have him with us. My mother and I are taking him to a big auction."

"An auction!" exclaimed Rema. "That's so smart. I wanted to have an auction for Snow White. I didn't make enough money selling her to Lulu."

"Mr. Olson set a fair price," said Lulu.

"And Snow White has a great home and owner," added Pam.

"You're lucky that Snow White still lives so close to you," Mark told Rema.

Rema smiled at Mark and patted Snow White. "My sweet old pony," she said.

Anna glared at Rema. She knew that Rema didn't care about Snow White anymore. Rema was just showing off for Mark.

Mark rubbed Lightning's upside-down heart marking. "You guys all have beautiful ponies," he said.

"Can we bring Snow White over to Snowflake now?" asked Lulu.

"Sure," said Mark.

Mark and Rema walked ahead to the paddock to get Snowflake. The Pony Pals followed with their ponies. When they were close to the paddock, Snow White gave a happy little whinny.

"I bet she already recognizes her son," said Anna.

"Keep Snow White outside for now," said Mark.

Snow White stretched her neck over the fence to sniff her son. Snowflake squealed, stamped his foot, and his ears went back. Lulu saw his big teeth bite into Snow White's neck.

Snow White squealed and pulled on her lead rope. She wanted to bite Snowflake back. Lulu yanked her away from the fence. Mark got a hold on Snowflake's halter and pulled Snowflake away.

"Oh, Snow White," cried Lulu. "Are you okay?" Lulu looked at Snow White's neck. "The skin isn't broken," she told Pam and Anna.

"Then she's all right," said Pam.

"Doesn't Snowflake know his own mother?" asked Anna.

"They've been separated for a long time," said Pam. "He didn't recognize her."

Mark led Snowflake to the other side of the paddock. Snowflake went back to grazing, and Mark came over to the Pony Pals.

"Sorry," he told them. "Snowflake doesn't usually act like that."

"Maybe they need time to get used to each other again," said Anna.

"It might help if there weren't any other ponies around," suggested Pam. "Maybe Anna and I should take our ponies away."

"That's a good idea," agreed Mark.

"We can ride over to Olson's horse farm," Pam told Anna. "You can interview Mr. Olson about Acorn."

"And I want to interview you about Snow White," Lulu told Mark. "Will you answer some questions about when Snow White was little? I'm writing the story of her life."

"We're all writing our ponies' biographies," said Pam.

"That's a good idea," said Mark. "I'd love to help you." Lulu noticed that he had a great smile.

"I'll help you, too, Lulu," said Rema. "I know a lot about Snow White."

Anna gave Rema a long look. Rema didn't

want to help Lulu. She wanted Mark to think she's a nice person. What a phony!

Lulu took out her Pony Pal notebook. She was ready to do the interview. But she was disappointed that Snowflake didn't like Snow White. Lulu wanted *Snow White's Story* to be full of happy things. Now she wondered, is Snow White's life story going to be sad?

A Long List

Anna and Pam rode their ponies down Lilac Lane. "Lulu's so lucky that she met Snow White's first owner," Anna said.

"And that he's nice," said Pam. "I hope we have good luck, too." Pam and Anna turned onto Mudge Road and headed toward Mr. Olson's horse farm.

Half an hour later, Anna and Pam were following Mr. Olson into his office. "A book about Acorn?" he said. "That sounds like a fine idea to me. I'll give you a list of all his owners."

Mr. Olson hit a few keys on his computer and printed out a page. He handed it to Anna. She counted the names. "Acorn has had eight different owners," she said.

"He's moved around a lot," said Mr. Olson.

"He's never going to have to move again," said Anna. "Unless it's with me."

"So he'll be a Pony Pal forever?" said Mr. Olson with a smile.

"That's right," said Anna.

Mr. Olson looked at the list. "Most of these folks have moved to other parts of the country," he said. "I've lost track of a lot of them." He pointed to a name. "You could start with Tommy Rand. He had Acorn for a couple of years and he lives in Wiggins."

"Not Tommy Rand!" exclaimed Anna.

"Anna asked Tommy about Acorn once," said Pam. "But he wouldn't tell her anything."

"Tommy's always mean to us," explained Anna. "He thinks he's a big shot. He doesn't want anyone to know that he had a little pony."

"I see," said Mr. Olson. He pointed to another name on the list. "Then try Sally Southack. She owned Acorn the longest of any of his owners."

"Does she live in Wiggins?" Pam asked.

Mr. Olson shook his head. "No, but she lives in a town near here. I have her phone number if you want."

"That'd be great," said Anna.

Mr. Olson hit more keys on his computer. He read Sally Southack's phone number off the screen. Anna wrote it down in her Pony Pal notebook.

"Now I want to ask you some questions," Anna told Mr. Olson. "Where was Acorn born?"

"Right on this farm," he said. "His mother was my childhood pony."

Anna asked Mr. Olson a lot of questions about when Acorn was little. Pam was happy that Anna had someone to talk to about Acorn. She couldn't wait to do some work on *Lightning's Story*.

When Pam got home she looked for her mother. Mrs. Crandal was talking on the phone in the barn office. She smiled at Pam and handed her some papers from the desk. Pam saw that they were Lightning's registration papers. She ran outside and leaned on the paddock fence to read them.

Lightning came over to the fence to see what Pam was doing. Pam looked up at her beautiful Connemara pony. "Lightning!" she exclaimed. "You were born in Ireland! I can't wait to tell Anna and Lulu." She went back to the office to ask her mother if she could invite Anna and Lulu for another barn sleepover.

An hour later Pam saw Lulu and Anna riding out of Pony Pal Trail. Pam and Lightning ran across the field to meet them.

"Guess what!?" exclaimed Pam. "Lightning was born in Ireland!"

"Wow!" said Anna.

"That's so cool," said Lulu.

"And my mother said we can use her computer for our pony stories," she told them.

"Let's go up to the hayloft now and have a meeting," said Lulu.

"And let's sleep in the hayloft tonight," said Anna.

"Perfect," said Lulu.

The Pony Pals took off Acorn's and Snow White's saddles and bridles and brought them to the barn. Then they climbed the ladder to the hayloft and sat around their hay bale table.

"The Pony Pal meeting about our Pony Pal Project will now come to order," said Anna in a pretend-serious voice.

The three girls giggled.

"Lulu, what happened with Snow White and Snowflake after we left?" asked Pam.

"Mark was great," said Lulu. "He held Snow White by the lead rope and let her graze closer and closer to the paddock fence. At first Snowflake ignored her. But

after a while he came over to the fence. His ears were forward and he whinnied at Snow White."

"What did Snow White do?" asked Pam.

"She whinnied back," Lulu said. "Then she went over to the fence and they sniffed each other."

"I'm glad they're not fighting anymore," said Pam.

"Me, too," said Lulu.

"Snow White and Snowflake are having a play date tomorrow," Anna told Pam.

"And Mark gave me pictures for *Snow White's Story*," Lulu said. She showed the photos to her friends. "Rema showed me all the ribbons she won with Snow White," she added.

"Rema just wanted to impress Mark," said Anna.

"I know," said Lulu. "But it's a good story for Snow White's book."

"Did you call Ms. Southack?" Pam asked Anna.

Anna nodded. "She was really nice to me on the phone," she said. "She's coming to see Acorn tomorrow. I'm going to interview her."

"And I'm going to fax a letter to Mr. O'Connor at Echo Farm," said Pam. "I'll ask him questions about Lightning."

"That's a good idea," said Anna.

The girls were still talking about their Pony Pal Project when they slipped into their sleeping bags that night.

"So far this is fun," Anna said as she drifted off to sleep.

"I love being a Pony Pal," mumbled Pam as she closed her eyes.

"Me, too," Lulu said. But Lulu didn't close her eyes. She was still wide-awake. She kept thinking about Snow White. Lulu quietly got up and made her way through the dark barn to the office. She sat in front of the computer and turned it on. Next, Lulu opened a file, named it SW.DOC, and started to write her pony's story.

SNOW WHITE'S STORY

by Lulu Sanders

Snow White was born at Valley Farm in New York State. Her mother's name was Rosey Ride and her father's name was Storm. Snow White's first owners were the Johnson family. Mark Johnson said, "Snow White was a playful and intelligent filly."

When Snow White was three years old, she had a foal named Snowflake. He was born in the barn at Valley Farm.

Snow White was an excellent mother. Once, another horse tried to hurt Snowflake. Snow White fought the attacker. Snow White has a scar on her right flank from that fight. Snowflake wasn't hurt because his mother protected him.

When Snowflake was a year old, his mother was sold to the Baxters. The Johnsons sold Snow White because that's what they do — breed and sell Welsh horses and ponies.

Rema Baxter bought Snow White. She loved her pony and rode it in many competitions. "I won a lot of ribbons with Snow White," Rema told me. "We were always the best-looking pair in the ring. Everyone said so. I only sold Snow White to Lulu because I grew too big for her."

After Rema had Snow White for four years, she moved to Wiggins. She took Snow White with her. But Rema didn't stay in Wiggins with her pony. She went to boarding school.

Snow White was lonely. One day she got her leg caught in barbed wire. I saved her life. After that my father let me buy Snow White.

Snow White and I are best friends. I want to keep her, even when I get too big to ride her. Maybe Snow White can be a driving pony like her best friend Acorn.

Crutches

The next morning the Pony Pals rode their ponies to Off-Main Diner for breakfast. Anna's mother owned the diner, so the Pony Pals could eat there for free. Pam wrote their food order and gave it to the cook. Anna and Lulu poured the juice. Then the three girls went to their favorite booth.

"Are you sure the fax I sent Mr. O'Connor is okay?" asked Pam.

"Let me read it again," said Lulu.

Pam took a folded piece of paper from

her Pony Pal notebook and handed it to
Lulu. Lulu read it out loud.

Dear Mr. O'Connor:

My name is Pam Crandal. Four years ago
my mother and father bought a Connemara pony from you. The pony's name is
Lightning and she is mine. I am trying to
learn everything I can about Lightning's
life. I want to write it all down.

I have a lot of questions about Lightning. For example, How did Lightning come
to the United States? What was her life
like in Ireland? I have other questions, too.

Please let me know if I can interview you
on the telephone. You can send me a fax at
203-555-0178 or telephone me at 203-
555-0172.

Thank you.

Sincerely,

Pamela Crandal

"It's perfect," said Anna.

"You write the best letters, Pam," said Lulu.

"Thanks," said Pam. "I want to write to the people who owned Lightning in Ireland, too."

The cook yelled from the kitchen, "Three Pony Pal Pancake Specials on deck!"

The girls went to pick up their orders. A raw carrot lay across each pile of blueberry pancakes. They laughed and thanked the cook.

Anna held up her carrot. "I guess this is the 'special' part of the Pony Pal Pancake Special," she said.

"It's the 'Pony' part, too," giggled Lulu.

While the Pony Pals ate their pancakes they talked about the day ahead. "I'm going to stay at the Baxters' while Snowflake and Snow White have their play date," said Lulu. "I like seeing them together."

"I'm going to interview Ms. Southack," said Anna.

"I'll go with you, Anna," said Pam. "I can be your secretary."

"That'd be great," said Anna.

The girls finished eating and brought the carrots out to their ponies. Anna put her arm around Acorn's neck. "I hope you recognize Ms. Southack," she told him.

Pam thought she heard a familiar *clip-clop* in the distance. She ran to the road and looked toward Main Street. A pretty woman with long dark hair was driving a black Morgan pony along Belgo Road.

"It's Ms. Wiggins and Beauty!" Pam called to Anna and Lulu. They ran to the road and stood beside Pam. The three girls waved to Ms. Wiggins. She waved back.

Ms. Wiggins was a good friend of the Pony Pals. She lived on a big estate that had wonderful riding trails. The Pony Pals could ride there anytime they wanted.

Ms. Wiggins stopped the pony cart in front of them.

"Beauty looks so beautiful!" exclaimed Anna.

Pam rubbed Beauty's sleek black neck. "She's put on weight," she said. Pam remembered how terrible Beauty looked when she first saw her. Beauty had been wild and half-starved from spending a winter outside alone. The Pony Pals and Lightning saved Beauty's life and Ms. Wiggins bought him.

"She's a great driving pony," said Ms. Wiggins. "I'm bringing her over to show Mr. Olson. Why don't you three ride your ponies over there with us?"

"We can't today," Anna told Ms. Wiggins. "We're too busy."

"What are you all so busy about?" asked Ms. Wiggins.

The Pony Pals told Ms. Wiggins about their Pony Pal Project to write about the lives of their ponies.

"That's a wonderful idea!" she exclaimed. "I hope you'll show them to me."

The girls promised they would and Ms.

Wiggins drove off. "See you soon," she shouted over her shoulder.

Anna looked at her watch. "We better hurry," she said. "I want to give Acorn a special grooming before Ms. Southack comes."

The girls rode their ponies to the corner of Belgo Road and Main Street. Lulu turned right to go to the Baxters'. Pam and Anna turned left to go to Anna's.

After Pam and Anna groomed Acorn, they went into the house to wait for Ms. Southack.

"Let's make her a snack," suggested Pam.

"Good idea," said Anna. Pam was putting out a plate of cookies and Anna was stirring lemonade when they heard a car come in the driveway.

Pam ran to the window. "Anna, come here," she called. "Quick."

Anna ran to the window and stood beside Pam. She saw a blond-haired woman getting out of a blue car. The woman's arms were in metal crutches. She leaned on the crutches and took a few slow steps.

"What happened to her legs?" Anna whispered.

"Maybe she fell off a horse," said Pam.

"That would be so awful," said Anna. Her heart beat faster. Did Ms. Southack get hurt falling off Acorn? Were her legs like that because of her pony?

Acorn and Sally

Sally Southack moved toward the paddock on her crutches.

The girls ran out of the house and down the driveway. "Hi," Anna called to Ms. Southack.

The woman turned around and smiled. "Hi," she said. "I'm Sally. Which one of you is Anna?"

"I am," said Anna. "This is my friend Pam."

"Hello," said Pam.

"Does that other pretty pony belong to you, Pam?" Ms. Southack asked.

"Yes," answered Pam. "Her name is Lightning. She's a Connemara pony and was born in Ireland."

"How interesting," said Ms. Southack. She moved her crutches forward and pulled her legs up to them.

Pam ran ahead to open the paddock gate and they all went inside.

"Can I help you, Ms. Southack?" asked Anna.

"I'm fine," said Ms. Southack with a smile. "Don't you worry. I'll ask for help if I need it. And call me 'Sally.'"

"Okay . . . Sally," said Anna, smiling.

"Acorn!" yelled Sally. Acorn looked up. "Acorn, get yourself over here!"

Acorn didn't play Catch-Me-If-You-Can with Sally. He came right over to her. Anna felt proud of her pony.

Sally blew on Acorn's nose. Acorn sniffed and nickered softly. Anna was sure that he recognized his old owner. Sally rubbed her cheek against his face. "Oh, Acorn," she said. "You were my very best friend." Anna saw tears in her eyes.

Sally held a crutch out to Pam. "Could you hold this for a minute?" she asked. Pam took the crutch. Sally leaned on the other crutch and stroked Acorn's face and neck. "My sweet pony," she said. "We had so much fun together. I loved riding you."

"Acorn's a good driving pony, too," Anna told Sally. "He's in parades. He was even in the circus."

"I would love to have seen that," said Sally.

"I can show you pictures," Anna told her.

"I drove him, too," Sally said. "But mostly I rode him. I brought some photos for you." She took the crutch back from Pam.

"Do you want to go inside and have some lemonade and cookies?" Anna asked Sally.

"I'd rather stay out here near my old friend," Sally answered. She looked around

and noticed the Harleys' picnic table. "Why don't we sit there," she suggested.

Pam went to the kitchen to get the snack. Anna went to her bedroom for her Pony Pal notebook and pictures of Acorn in the circus. Sally stayed with Acorn.

A few minutes later the two girls and Sally were sitting at the picnic table. Anna handed Pam her notebook and a pencil. "Pam is going to write down what you say about Acorn," Anna told Sally. "It's hard for me to listen and write at the same time. I'm dyslexic."

"I bet you're a good artist, though," said Sally.

"Anna is a great artist," said Pam.

"I wish I was good at reading and writing, too," said Anna.

"That's the way it goes," said Sally. She patted her own legs. "Some parts of our bodies and minds work better than other parts."

"Did you fall off a horse?" Anna blurted out. She felt her face get red. She was embarrassed by her own question.

Sally smiled at her. "No," she said. "I have cerebral palsy. I was born this way. "

"I'm glad you didn't fall off Acorn," Anna told her.

"Oh, I fell off that pony plenty," Sally said with a laugh. "But that's not what went wrong with my legs. Acorn was the best thing that ever happened to me when I was a little girl."

"Me, too," said Anna.

Anna and Sally smiled at each other. "I have lots more questions," Anna said.

"Good," said Sally. "I love to talk about Acorn."

Anna asked Sally questions and Pam wrote down the answers.

When they were finished, Sally had a question for Anna. "Do you know any of the other people who have owned Acorn?" she asked.

"One more," said Anna. "His name is Tommy Rand. But he's a mean kid."

"Tommy Rand," said Sally thoughtfully. "I remember seeing him in a parade with

Acorn once. He seemed like a sweet little boy to me."

"He's not little anymore," said Anna. "And he's not sweet."

"That's too bad," said Sally.

"What kind of parade was Tommy in?" asked Pam.

"A costume parade," said Sally. "Tommy was dressed like a teddy bear. He was very cute."

"Tommy Rand as a teddy bear!" said Pam. "I'd love to see that."

"You should interview him," Sally told Anna. "Maybe he has a picture from the costume parade."

"That would be so much fun to see," giggled Anna.

Ms. Southack pulled a Polaroid camera from her bag. "Pam, would you take a picture of Anna and me with Acorn?" she said.

"Sure," said Pam.

"Can she take two?" asked Anna. "So I can have one for my story about Acorn."

"Of course," said Ms. Southack. "And I'd like a copy of *Acorn's Story* when it's finished."

"Okay," said Anna. "I'm going to write the part about you today."

After Sally left, Anna said good-bye to Pam and ran upstairs to her room. She couldn't wait to work on *Acorn's Story*. She already had some ideas for the drawings she wanted to do for it.

ACORN'S STORY

by Anna Harley

Acorn was born on Mr. Olson's horse farm in Wiggins, Connecticut. His mother's name was Mushroom and his father's name was Jumper.

Mr. Olson said, "Acorn was always a smart pony. And he wasn't afraid of anything."

Acorn had eight different homes. I don't think he minded. He likes to meet new people and do new things.

When Acorn was five years old, Sally Southack bought him. Sally couldn't walk. She used a wheelchair to get around. But she learned to ride Acorn. She said, "I could move as fast as the other children when we had our riding lessons. That made me feel good.

"After some operations I learned to walk with crutches. I loved having Acorn as a pet and for riding."

Sally told me some of the cute things Acorn did when Sally was a little girl.

She said that Acorn liked to played tag.

He also won first prize in a pet show.

Sally told me that Acorn always wanted to go inside the house.

Sally Southack had Acorn for eight years. Then she sold Acorn back to Mr. Olson. She couldn't keep him because she was moving to a big city with her mother and father.

Now Sally is married and lives in the country. She has a big Thoroughbred horse named Like The Wind.

Sally still loves Acorn. She said, "I owe my love of horses and my ability to ride to Acorn. I will never forget him."

Pam's E-mail

That night Pam worked on *Lightning's Story*. She started by looking up Connemara ponies in the encyclopedia. She read the article and wrote what she learned in her Pony Pal notebook.

1. Connemara ponies have lived in Ireland for hundreds of years.

2. The land in Connemara is rugged. The weather is rainy and windy.

3. Connemara ponies live like goats in the hills.

4. There is not much for the ponies in Connemara to eat. Sometimes they eat seaweed.
5. Connemara ponies have very strong legs and are great jumpers.
6. Connemara ponies make good farm ponies. They are hard workers.
7. The Irish people are proud of their strong, smart ponies.

Pam closed the notebook and then she went out to see Lightning. She took an apple out of her pocket and held it out to her pony. Pam smiled as she felt Lightning's soft lips against her hand. She hugged her pony. "I'm glad you came to America," she said.

As Pam was walking back into the house the phone was ringing. She picked up the receiver and said, "Crandal residence."

"This is Richard O'Connor from Echo Farm," the voice on the other end said. "Is Pam Crandal there?"

"I'm Pam," she said. "I want to ask you some questions about Lightning."

"I know," Mr. O'Connor said. "I received your fax and I'm happy to help you."

Pam pulled her Pony Pal notebook out of her pocket. She was going to learn the answers to her questions about Lightning! Wait until she told Anna and Lulu!

The next morning Anna and Lulu rode to Pam's on Pony Pal Trail.

"Snowflake and Snow White had a great time together yesterday," Lulu told Anna. "They raced along the side of the fence and grazed side by side. Snowflake copied everything Snow White did, just like a foal. They even scratched one another's withers with their teeth. It was so cute."

"When is Snowflake leaving?" asked Anna.

"Tomorrow," said Lulu sadly. "I wish he didn't have to go. He's a great pony."

Anna and Lulu came to the end of Pony Pal Trail and galloped their mounts across the Crandals' big field. They saw Pam and Lightning in the riding ring. Lightning cleared three high jumps in a row.

"That was beautiful!" Anna called to Pam.

Pam walked Lightning over to them.

"You could win a lot of ribbons with jumping like that," said Lulu.

Pam patted her pony's sweaty neck. "*Lightning* would win the ribbons," she said. "She's the star."

The girls put their ponies out in the field. While the ponies grazed, the Pony Pals sat on the big rock to talk.

Pam told Anna and Lulu about her telephone interview with Mr. O'Connor. "Lightning came in an airplane from Ireland," she said. "Mr. O'Connor's sending me pictures of it."

"That's neat," said Anna.

"He also told me that Lightning was in the mountains," said Pam. "She roamed free with other Connemara ponies."

"Lightning was a wild pony!" exclaimed Anna. "Wow!"

"Maybe Lightning should have been left in the wild," said Pam. "She would have been free."

"Who captured her?" asked Lulu.

"A company called Kelly Connemaras," answered Pam. "They round up the Connemara ponies from their land and sell them to people all over the world. Mr. O'Connor gave me Mr. Kelly's E-mail address. I sent him a message early this morning."

"Let's go see if Mr. Kelly wrote back to you," said Lulu.

The three girls ran to the barn office. "I've never used E-mail," said Anna.

"It's easy," said Pam. "You'll see."

Pam turned on the computer in the barn office and checked the Internet to see if she had any E-mail. "Look!" said Pam. "I have a message." Pam hit some keys on the computer and the message from Mr. Kelly came up on the screen.

I am glad that you have one of our lovely Connemaras, Miss Crandal. I remember your pony. Who could forget that heart marking? It was so big on that wee forehead. She was a thin creature. We had some very hard weather that year and there wasn't much for the ponies to eat. If we had not caught your pony she could have starved during the very long winter.

Lightning is a perfect name for her. She was the fastest yearling in the roundup. We would call her *Lasrachai*, which is the way we say *Lightning* in our Gaelic language.

You have yourself a fine pony.

All the best from Connemara — land of fine horses and ponies. Ryan Kelly.

"Poor Lightning," said Anna. "She didn't have enough to eat when she was little."

"It sounds like she had a hard life in Connemara," said Lulu.

"Now I'm glad she was captured," said Pam.

Anna put a hand on Pam's shoulder. "Me, too," she said.

"I'm going to print out Mr. Kelly's E-mail letter," said Pam. "I'll put it in *Lightning's Story*." Pam turned on the printer and hit a few more keys on the computer.

"When she was a baby, Lightning's upside-down heart was as big as it is now," said Anna. "That must have looked so cute."

"Will you draw me a picture of Lightning as a foal?" asked Pam.

"Sure," said Anna.

"Anna wrote *Acorn's Story* last night," Lulu told Pam.

"But I'm going to write more," Anna said. "I'm going to interview one more person."

"Who?" asked Pam.

Anna grinned. "It's someone you know," she said.

"Tommy Rand!?" shrieked Lulu.

"I can't believe he agreed to an interview," said Pam.

"He didn't," said Anna. "I'm going to interview his mother. I already asked her."

"That's brilliant," giggled Lulu.

"Will you come with me?" Anna asked.

"Sure!" said Pam and Lulu together.

"Learning about our ponies is a lot of fun," added Pam.

"Wait until Tommy Rand finds out that Anna is going to write about him!" said Lulu with a giggle.

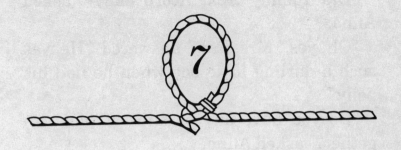

Tommy-the-Pooh

The Pony Pals rode up North Street until they came to the dirt road that led to the Rands'. After a half mile they came to the Rands' house. Tommy's mother was weeding her front garden. She waved to the Pony Pals and came over to talk to them. The girls dismounted.

"It's such a lovely idea that you girls are writing about your ponies," she said. She rubbed Acorn's nuzzle. He nickered softly. "I'm happy to talk about Tommy and this sweet pony."

"Did Tommy treat Acorn okay?" asked Anna.

"Oh, yes," Mrs. Rand answered. "He was such a darling little boy when he had his pony."

"Do you have any pictures of them to-gether?" asked Anna.

"I have," she said. "I'll go get them."

In a minute Mrs. Rand was back with a pile of photos. In some pictures Tommy was on Acorn's back. In others he was hugging the pony. Anna couldn't believe it was the same Tommy Rand she knew.

"This is the best one," said Mrs. Rand. She held up a photo. Tommy was in a bear costume and Acorn wore floppy donkey ears.

"Tommy is Winnie-the-Pooh and Acorn is Eeyore!" exclaimed Lulu.

"Acorn looks so cute," said Pam.

"So does Tommy," added Anna with a gig-gle.

"They won first prize," said Mrs. Rand. "You can have that picture for your story about Acorn. I have another copy."

"Thanks," said Anna. She took the photo.

"Will you make a copy of *Acorn's Story* for us?" Mrs. Rand asked Anna. "I'm sure Tommy would love to have it."

"Sure," said Anna. But she didn't think Tommy would want *Acorn's Story*. Especially if it had a picture of him as a teddy bear in it.

The Pony Pals said good-bye to Mrs. Rand and rode away. Before long they saw Tommy Rand speeding toward them on his mountain bike. He screeched to a stop in front of them. Lightning and Snow White spooked and backed away. But Acorn didn't mind the bike at all.

"What are the Pony *Pests* doing on my road?" Tommy asked in a mean voice.

"We were talking to your mother about you and Acorn," Pam told him. "Anna is writing Acorn's life story."

"Everyone wants to see the book when she's finished," added Lulu.

"Your mother gave me a cute picture of

you as Winnie-the-Pooh," said Anna. "I'm going to put it in the book."

"Hey!" shouted Tommy. "Give me that picture. That's mine. Hand it over, Pony Pest."

"If you call me Pony Pest," said Anna, "I'm going to call you Tommy-the-Pooh."

Tommy dropped his bike and came toward the Pony Pals. He was very angry. Anna's heart pounded. Would he try to hurt them? Would he hurt Acorn?

"Let's go!" shouted Pam. She moved Lightning into a canter. Lulu followed on Snow White.

Tommy reached up to grab Anna. She tapped Acorn with her heel and he burst into a canter.

Anna heard Tommy shouting after them. He was trying to catch them on his bike. "Faster, Acorn!" Anna called to her pony. "Faster!"

The girls didn't slow their ponies down until they came to the end of the dirt road.

Anna looked back. Tommy wasn't behind them anymore. "He gave up," she told Pam and Lulu.

"All-*right!*" the Pony Pals shouted.

"Let's go to my house for lunch," said Anna.

"Our ponies could use a rest." Lulu said. "And I'm hungry."

Back at the Harleys', Pam and Lulu made lunch while Anna wrote another chapter for *Acorn's Story* on her computer.

Tommy Rand is another person who owned Acorn. Tommy had Acorn for only two years. He and Acorn played together and Tommy learned to ride on Acorn. "Tommy loved Acorn so much," said Tommy's mother. "That boy would cry like a baby if we wouldn't let him play with his pony."

Acorn and Tommy won a prize in a costume parade. Here is their picture.

Acorn is my best friend. I can tell him all of my problems. I never want Acorn to have another owner. He will stay with me forever.

A Pony Pal Problem

The ponies munched on hay in the Harley paddock while the girls ate peanut butter and jelly sandwiches at the picnic table. They talked about Tommy Rand and their escape from him. But Pam could see that Lulu wasn't happy.

"Lulu, what's wrong?" she asked.

"I wish we could keep Snowflake," said Lulu sadly. "He and Snow White are getting along so great. It's like he's part of the Pony Pals and now he's going away. We don't even know who will buy him."

"Ask your dad to buy him for you and Snow White," suggested Anna.

"I can't ask my dad," said Lulu. "He's in India."

"You can telephone him," said Pam.

"He's tracking elephants in the jungle," said Lulu. "There aren't any phones there."

"What about your grandmother?" asked Anna. "Maybe she'll buy him for you."

"My grandmother would *never* buy a pony," said Lulu. "She didn't want me to have Snow White."

"I have an idea," said Anna. "Pam's mother could buy Snowflake and use him in her riding school."

"That's a good idea," said Lulu. "Then we would see him all the time."

"She doesn't need any more ponies," said Pam. "She just bought Splash and Daisy. But we could ask her."

"It's worth a try," said Anna.

Lulu stood up. "Let's do it right now."

The girls rode Pony Pal Trail to the Crandals'. Mrs. Crandal was giving a private lesson in the riding ring. The Pony Pals sat on a big rock and waited for the lesson to end. But when that student finished, there was another lesson with two more students. One rode Daisy and the other rode Splash.

"If your mother had another school pony she could teach three kids at a time," Lulu said to Pam.

"We should tell her that," said Anna.

"And tell her that we'd help her train Snowflake to be a school pony," said Lulu. "The way we trained Daisy and Splash."

Pam took out her Pony Pal notebook and pencil. "I'm going to write those ideas down. We need a Pony Pal Plan for asking Mom to buy Snowflake."

When Mrs. Crandal's riding lesson was finished, the three girls ran over to Mrs. Crandal and the two ponies. It was time to put their Pony Pal Plan into action. "Anna and I can bring Daisy and Splash to the barn and take off their tack for you," Lulu told her.

"And cool them down," added Anna.

"Thank you, girls," Mrs. Crandal said. "That's very sweet of you."

Anna took Daisy's reins and Lulu took Splash's.

Mrs. Crandal headed toward the barn. "I'll be in my office if you need me," she said.

"Wait up, Mom," Pam called. "I need to talk to you." Pam and her mother went into the barn together. Anna showed Lulu that her fingers were crossed. Lulu crossed her fingers, too.

While Lulu cooled Splash down with a big sponge, she thought about Snowflake. She hoped with all her heart that the next day Snowflake would belong to the Crandals.

Anna and Lulu were turning Splash and Daisy out in the pasture when Pam came out of the barn. She looked discouraged. "My mom said she has all the ponies and all the students she can handle," Pam told Anna and Lulu.

"Did you tell her we'd take care of Snowflake?" asked Lulu.

Pam nodded. "She still won't buy him," she said.

"There she is," said Lulu. Mrs. Crandal was walking toward the Pony Pals.

"Maybe she changed her mind," whispered Anna.

Lulu crossed her fingers again.

"Thanks for taking care of Splash and Daisy for me," Mrs. Crandal told Lulu and Anna. She put a hand on Lulu's arm. "I'm sorry I can't buy Snowflake."

Lulu was very disappointed, but she understood Mrs. Crandal couldn't buy another pony. "That's okay, Mrs. Crandal," she said.

That night the Pony Pals had another barn sleepover. After a picnic dinner in the hayloft, they went to the barn office to work on their pony stories.

Pam wrote *Lightning's Story* on the computer while Anna drew pictures for her.

Lulu tried to write about how Snow White and Snowflake met again and then were separated. But it made her sad, so she stopped. The next day Snowflake was leaving forever. Lulu closed her Pony Pal notebook and went to see what Pam had written.

LIGHTNING'S STORY

by Pam Crandal

Lightning is a Connemara pony. She comes from a place called Connemara. Connemara is in northwestern Ireland. It is a rocky, rough land between the Atlantic Ocean and a lake called Lough Corrib.

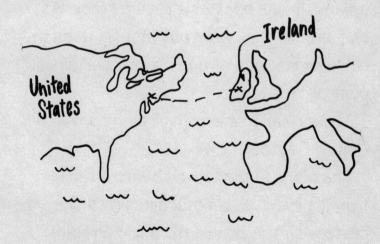

Lightning has had two owners besides me. A horse dealer from Ireland named Ryan Kelly and Mr. Richard O'Connor of Echo Farm in America.

Mr. Kelly lets his ponies roam free on his mountain. He brought Lightning off the mountain when she was a yearling.

That year Mr. O'Connor ordered three Connemara ponies from Mr. Kelly. One of them was Lightning.

The three ponies were driven to Dublin, Ireland, in the back of a pickup truck. At the airport they were put in a big wooden box. The box was swung up into the airplane with a crane.

The airplane flew from Ireland to the United States.

The plane landed at Stewart International airport. A big machine lifted the crate with the ponies from the airplane.

The ponies were unloaded from the box and put in stalls in a barn at the airport. They had to stay there for three days. That was to be sure that they didn't bring any disease from Ireland.

Mr. O'Connor picked up his three ponies at the airport and drove them to Echo Farm in a horse trailer.

Mr. O'Connor says, "Lightning was a skinny thing. But she was fast. That's why we named her Lightning. And with good care and food, she soon looked great."

Mr. O'Connor also said, "Lightning was easy to train. She's a sweetheart of a pony. No wonder she has that little up-side-down heart on her forehead."

Echo Farm used Lightning in their riding

and always won ribbons in the jumping class and cross-country classes.

I bought Lightning from Mr. O'Connor.

Lightning is a wonderful jumper. When I jump with her it feels like we're flying. I am going be in more horse shows with Lightning. She likes the excitement. And she loves to jump.

Lightning loves other animals and wants to protect them. She protected Fat Cat's kittens when they were born. And she and our dog, Woolie, are best friends.

I wish everyone in the world could have a pony as special as Lightning.

The Authors' Table

At breakfast the next morning the Pony Pals talked about their pony stories.

"Let's make copies of them today," said Pam.

"We can do it at the library," said Lulu.

After breakfast, the girls rode their ponies to the Harley's. They put the ponies in the paddock and walked across the town green to the library.

"How many copies should we make?" asked Lulu.

"I want to send one to Mr. Kelly in Ireland and one to Echo Farm," said Pam.

"I'm making a copy for the Johnsons and one for the Baxters," said Lulu.

"I need two copies of mine, too," said Anna.

Lulu opened the heavy front door to the library and they went in. The librarian, Mrs. Elliot, was at the front desk. "Hello, girls," she said. "Let me know if I can help you find books."

"We wrote our own book," said Anna.

"About our ponies," added Lulu.

"We want to make copies on the library's copy machine," added Pam.

Anna jingled the coins in her pocket. "We need to make a lot of copies," she said.

"You wrote your own stories!" exclaimed Mrs. Elliot. "I'd love to see them." The Pony Pals showed her the stories of their ponies.

"I'm very impressed with your work," said Mrs. Elliot. "This summer I have a special table in the library for books by local authors. We call it the Authors' Table. Why don't you put your three stories together in one book? Then I'll put it out on the table."

"My grandmother will love that," said Lulu.

"So will Tommy Rand," said Anna with a giggle.

"If you make a copy for the library," said Mrs. Elliot, "you can make your own copies for free."

"It's a deal," said Pam.

The girls went to the copy machine in the back room.

"We started writing about our ponies because Snowflake was coming to Wiggins," said Anna. "Now he's leaving and our stories are finished."

"I still wish we could find someone we know to buy Snowflake," said Pam.

"It's hopeless," said Lulu. She felt so sad she wanted to cry.

Lulu and Pam copied their stories while Anna made a cover for their book.

Lives of the Ponies
by the Pony Pals
Pam Crandal,
Anna Harley, and
Lulu Sanders

The Pony Pals had just finished when Ms. Wiggins came into the library. She didn't see the Pony Pals, but they saw her.

"It's Ms. Wiggins," said Lulu.

"Maybe we can get *her* to buy Snowflake!" exclaimed Anna.

"She just bought Beauty," said Lulu. "We can't ask her to buy *another* pony."

"Why not?" said Anna. "She's got plenty of room."

"And Mr. Silver helps her take care of her animals," said Pam.

"Come on," said Anna. "Let's ask her."

"Show her the picture of Snowflake," Pam told Lulu.

Lulu grabbed *Snow White's Story* from the copy machine. "We'll need all our Pony Pal Power for this one," she told her friends.

The Pony Pals went to the main part of the library. They waved to Ms. Wiggins.

"It's the Pony Pals," she said. "How are your stories about your ponies coming along?"

"We finished," said Pam.

"Show her yours," Anna said to Lulu. Lulu opened *Snow White's Story* to the picture of Snowflake and Snow White together.

"This is Snow White's son," said Lulu. She told Ms. Wiggins all about Snowflake and how the Johnsons were going to bring him to an auction.

"Snowflake is a *wonderful* pony," said

Anna. "The person who buys him is very lucky."

"You should see him, Ms. Wiggins," said Pam. "He's *very* special."

"If he's anything like his mother, he must be wonderful," said Ms. Wiggins.

"We're going over there now to say good-bye to him," said Lulu.

"Why don't you come see him for yourself," said Pam.

"I'd love to, girls," Ms. Wiggins said. "But an old friend is coming for a visit. I have to be home when she arrives."

"Can you come for just a minute?" asked Anna.

"It's your only chance to see Snow White's son," said Lulu.

Ms. Wiggins looked thoughtfully at the Pony Pals. She smiled. "I know what you three are up to," she said. "You want me to buy Snowflake."

"We know you'd love him," said Anna.

"I'm sorry, girls," Ms. Wiggins said. "But I can't take care of another pony right now."

The Pony Pals nodded. They understood. Ms. Wiggins said good-bye to the girls and left the library.

"We used all of our Pony Pal Power," said Lulu sadly. "It just didn't work this time."

Saying Good-bye

The Pony Pals went back to the library office to finish copying their pony stories. A few minutes later they put *Lives of the Ponies* on the Authors' table.

"Thank you, girls," Mrs. Elliot said. "A lot of people will be reading your book."

"Thank you for letting us use the copy machine," added Pam.

"If you write more chapters, bring them in," said Mrs. Elliot. "I can add them to your book."

"We will," said Lulu.

"I like being an author," added Anna.

The girls said good-bye to Mrs. Elliot and left the library. They crossed the town green to Anna's house. It was time to ride over to the Baxters' to say good-bye to Snowflake.

Half an hour later the Pony Pals were riding down Lilac Lane. Lulu leaned forward and patted Snow White's shoulder. "Snow White," she said sadly, "this is the last time you'll see your son."

Anna suddenly yelled, "Look! Ms. Wiggins's car is here!"

Lulu saw Ms. Wiggins's red car parked in the Baxters' driveway. "Maybe she changed her mind," Lulu called to Anna and Pam. "Maybe she'll buy Snowflake after all."

The Pony Pals galloped the rest of the way to the Baxters'. Ms. Wiggins saw them and waved. Mark waved, too.

Lulu counted three other people in the paddock besides Ms. Wiggins and Mark. Rema, Mark Johnson's mother, and a woman that Lulu didn't recognize.

The Pony Pals halted their ponies, dismounted, and led them toward the paddock. Snowflake saw Snow White and nickered a hello. Snow White strained at the reins to get closer to Snowflake. Lulu led her over to the fence and the two ponies sniffed one another's faces.

Lulu introduced Anna and Pam to Mrs. Johnson. And Ms. Wiggins introduced the girls and their ponies to the stranger. Her name was Sarah Morehouse.

"I've heard so much about you and your ponies," Ms. Morehouse told the Pony Pals.

"Snow White used to be my pony," said Rema proudly.

"Well, Snow White is a beautiful pony," said Ms. Morehouse.

"Snowflake is going to be all white someday," Mark said. "Like his mother."

Lulu crossed her fingers and hoped that Ms. Wiggins was going to buy Snowflake.

"Snowflake would look so pretty in a paddock with Picasso and Beauty," Anna told Ms. Wiggins.

"I'm not here to buy Snowflake," Ms. Wiggins said. "Sarah and I just wanted to see him."

Lulu could tell that Ms. Wiggins meant what she said. She felt disappointed all over again.

"Sarah and I have been best friends since we were children," Ms. Wiggins said. "We used to ride together the way you girls do. Sarah lives in Falls Town."

Anna noticed that Ms. Wiggins's friend was looking at Snowflake. "Snowflake is a lovely pony," Ms. Morehouse said as she rubbed his nose. She turned to Ms. Wiggins. "Do you think Alison would like him?"

"Alison would *love* him," said Ms. Wiggins.

"Who's Alison?" asked Anna.

"My daughter," Ms. Morehouse answered.

"And my goddaughter," said Ms. Wiggins. "She's a wonderful girl."

"Alison is at a sleep-away riding camp

this month," said Ms. Morehouse. "I've been looking for a pony for her."

The Pony Pals exchanged smiles. Pam whispered, "If Snowflake lives in Falls Town, we can see him." Lulu showed Anna and Pam that she had her fingers crossed.

"Has Snowflake done any driving?" Ms. Morehouse asked Mrs. Johnson.

"Oh, yes," answered Mrs. Johnson. "He's a fine driving pony."

"And he's a terrific trail-riding pony," added Mark.

"I'd love to see Alison riding on my trails," said Ms. Wiggins. "And I could teach her how to drive."

"Ms. Wiggins taught me how to drive," Anna told Ms. Morehouse. "She's the best teacher."

"I'm sure she is," said Ms. Morehouse. She turned to Mrs. Johnson. "I know you were going to sell Snowflake at an auction," she said. "But would you sell him to me instead?"

"I'd have to get the right price for him,"

said Mrs. Johnson. "But I do prefer to sell him to someone I've met."

Ms. Morehouse and Mrs. Johnson left the paddock to speak privately about Snowflake's price. The Pony Pals hit high fives and shouted, "All-*right*."

"Hold on," Ms. Wiggins told them. "Snowflake isn't Sarah's yet."

But when Ms. Morehouse and Mrs. Johnson came back in the paddock they were both smiling. "Well, it looks like Alison has a pony!" said Mrs. Johnson.

The Pony Pals cheered. Ms. Morehouse went over to Snowflake and looked him in the eye. "You'll make a wonderful pony for my wonderful daughter," she said.

"Can Alison be a Pony Pal when she and Snowflake visit me?" Ms. Wiggins asked the Pony Pals.

The Pony Pals looked at one another to be sure they agreed on the answer. "Yes," they said in unison.

"If you say Alison would make a good Pony Pal," said Pam, "it must be true."

"Snowflake will be a Pony Pal, too," said Lulu.

"We'll all have fun," added Anna.

"So everyone and every pony will be happy," said Mrs. Johnson with a smile. "Now where do we deliver this lucky pony?"

"Sarah is staying with me for a few days," Ms. Wiggins told Mrs. Johnson. "So you can bring Snowflake to my place."

"Mark and I can trailer him there now," Mrs. Johnson told Ms. Wiggins.

"And we'll ride over to welcome him," said Lulu.

Mark rubbed his hand along Snowflake's back. "I'd like to ride Snowflake," he said. "It would be more fun for him than being in the trailer. Besides, I want to ride him one last time."

"You can ride most of the way on trails," Pam told him.

"Cool," Mark said. "It would be fun to ride with the Pony Pals."

"It would!?" said Rema with surprise. She turned to face Mark.

"Don't you ride with them, Rema?" asked Mark.

"They're younger than me," Rema said, and tossed her head.

"That shouldn't make any difference," said Mark.

The Pony Pals smiled at one another. They all liked Mark.

Soon the Pony Pals and Mark were riding Pony Pal Trail toward the Wiggins Estate. Mark rode in front of Lulu and Snow White. Lulu saw that Snowflake had a steady, graceful gait. Just like Snow White, thought Lulu.

Lulu smiled to herself. She already had another chapter for *Snow White's Story* in *Lives of the Ponies*.

Dear Pam, Anna and Lulu,
I came home from
camp yesterday. I was
so surprised to see a
pony in my backyard!
I thought I was
dreaming. I finally have
my own pony. Snowflake
is the perfect pony for me.
I rode him right away.
I know we will be best
friends.

My mother said that
you will ride with me
when I visit Wiggins.

I can't wait to meet
you and Snowflake's
mother.

    Your friend,
    Alison

P.S. Aren't ponies the best?

P.P.S. Here's a drawing of me
and Snowflake.

Be a Pony Pal®!

**Anna, Pam, and Lulu want you to join them
on adventures with their favorite ponies!**

**Order now and you get a free pony portrait bookmark and two
collecting cards in all the books—for you *and* your pony pal!**

❏ BBC48583-0	#1 I Want a Pony	$2.99
❏ BBC48584-9	#2 A Pony for Keeps	$2.99
❏ BBC48585-7	#3 A Pony in Trouble	$2.99
❏ BBC48586-5	#4 Give Me Back My Pony	$2.99
❏ BBC25244-5	#5 Pony to the Rescue	$2.99
❏ BBC25245-3	#6 Too Many Ponies	$2.99
❏ BBC54338-5	#7 Runaway Pony	$2.99
❏ BBC54339-3	#8 Good-bye Pony	$2.99
❏ BBC62974-3	#9 The Wild Pony	$2.99
❏ BBC62975-1	#10 Don't Hurt My Pony	$2.99
❏ BBC86597-8	#11 Circus Pony	$2.99
❏ BBC86598-6	#12 Keep Out, Pony!	$2.99
❏ BBC86600-1	#13 The Girl Who Hated Ponies	$2.99
❏ BBC86601-X	#14 Pony-Sitters	$3.50
❏ BBC86632-X	#15 The Blind Pony	$3.50
❏ BBC74210-8	Pony Pals Super Special #1: The Baby Pony	$5.99

Available wherever you buy books, or use this order form.

ENTER THE TRIVIA SWEEPS!

One Lucky Winner!

GRAND PRIZE
6 months of FREE horseback riding lessons!

Answer these four Pony Pals trivia questions to enter:

1) What is Anna's pony's name?

_____

2) What do the Pony Pals call their riding trail?

_____

3) On whose estate do the Pony Pals often ride their ponies?

_____

4) What kind of pony is Lulu's pony, Snow White?

_____

YES! Enter me in the Pony Pals Trivia Sweeps!
I am including the answers to the 4 questions.

Circle One: Boy   Girl

Name_____Birth date _____

      First   Last   Mo./Day/Yr.

Address_____

City_____State_____Zip code_____

Please tell us where you got this book: Bookstore • Price Club • Book Club • Book Fair

Other_____